THE
FAVORITE DAUGHTER

ALLEN SAY

ARTHUR A. LEVINE BOOKS
AN IMPRINT OF SCHOLASTIC INC.

Library of Congress Cataloging-in-Publication Data
Say, Allen.
The favorite daughter / Allen Say. — 1st ed.   p. cm.
Summary: Yuriko, teased at school for her unusual name and Japanese ancestry, yearns
to be more ordinary until her father reminds her of how special she is.
ISBN 978-0-545-17662-0 (hardcover : alk. paper) 1. Japanese Americans—Juvenile fiction. [1. Japanese
Americans—Fiction. 2. Fathers and daughters—Fiction. 3. Teasing—Fiction. 4. Schools—Fiction. 5. Artists—
Fiction. 6. San Francisco (Calif.) —Fiction.] I. Title.
PZ7.S2744Fav 2013   [E] —dc23   2012026830

10 9 8 7 6 5 4 3 2 1   13 14 15 16 17
First edition, June 2013
Printed in Malaysia   108
The art for this book was created using watercolors, pen and ink, pencil, and two photos.
Book design by Allen Say and Charles Kreloff

For my daughter

Yuriko came to stay with her father on Thursday that week.

"Do you have any pictures of me when I was little?" she asked.

"I have a whole bunch, why?" Father asked.

"Mrs. Riley wants to make a class album."

"With baby pictures? What fun! Let's look after dinner."

"Remember this?" Father asked.
"My kimono! I loved it!"
"You sure ruined it in a hurry."
"I liked making art."

"That was the prettiest kimono I could find in Tokyo, and you made mud pies in it."

"It was Play-Doh, Daddy. And you went to Japan all by yourself."

"Sweetheart, you were only two at the time . . . a little too young for the trip. So how many pictures do you need for the album?"

"Just one. This is perfect."

The next morning, Father said, "Mrs. Riley is going to love your picture. I bet everybody will be jealous."

Yuriko smiled. "Jenny's mom is bringing me home today."

"Good. I'll see you at snack time."

When Yuriko came home, she went straight to her room.

"What happened?" Father asked.

"They all laughed at me."

"You mean at the picture? They were just teasing you."

"No. They said Japanese dolls have *black* hair. 'Yoo-REE-ko in ki-MO-na!' They sang it all day long. Ki-MO-na, Daddy! And the new art teacher called me 'Eureka.' So everybody calls me that now, even Josh and Tiffany."

"They called you that in kindergarten. . . ."

"I don't like it. I want an American name, Daddy."

"Like Suzy or Maggie? How about Louise?"

"No. I like Michelle."

"That's a French name, Honey."

"I don't care. Jennifer is okay too."

"Umm . . . feels like I'm getting a new daughter here. Tell you what, let's go out and talk about this."

"Can we go to Toraya?"

"Ah, Michelle likes sushi too." Father grinned.

"I haven't been here in ages," she said.

"About a month," said Father. "When you were still Yuriko."

"Yuriko-chan! How you've grown!" the man behind the counter exclaimed.

Father bowed. "Kudo-san, allow me to introduce my daughter Michelle."

"Michelle? You look exactly like Yuriko-chan. I didn't know you were twins."

"No, I'm Yuriko . . . I mean, I was . . . oh, bother, you can call me Yuriko."

"Good, it goes better with sushi, and I know what you like," Kudo-san said.

"Thank you." Father nodded.

"So, did you tell your art teacher how to pronounce your name?" Father asked.

"Mrs. Riley did. But it didn't do any good. I don't like school anymore. I don't like art either."

"It was a mistake, Sweetheart, and she probably feels awful. And the kids are only teasing you. Just ignore them."

Yuriko rubbed her chopsticks.

"Sharpening your sticks, eh? Where did you learn that trick?"

"Everybody does it. The lady over there was doing it."

"Well, it's bad manners," Father whispered.

"It's all right, Yuriko-chan, you can play with your chopsticks," Kudo-san said. "Here, take these."

"Thank you, Kudo-san!"

"Toraya souvenirs," Father said. "Take them to school and teach the kids how to use them properly."

"He gave me a lot," Yuriko said.

"Those are throwaways."

"I know, but I'm not going to throw them away. Mrs. Riley says we should recycle everything."

"Quite right," Father said. "How would you like to take a quick trip to Japan?"

"When?"

"Tomorrow."

"I can't, Daddy. Ms. Hobbs gave us an assignment. She's the new art teacher."

"What about?"

"We have to do something about the Golden Gate Bridge."

"She *is* new here. When is it due?"

"Monday. Everybody is drawing it. Art isn't fun anymore. It's all projects now. Teachers tell us what to do."

"Well, they're fun if you think of them as puzzles. And it's *really* fun when you come up with a cool solution."

"But I don't know what to do."

"You have a whole weekend, Sweetheart."

"But I can't go to Japan, Daddy."

"It's a real quick trip."

In the morning, Father drove Yuriko to Golden Gate Park.

"The Japanese Garden! I've been here before!"

"I told you it was going to be a quick trip. Let's see how much you remember."

"There's a funny bridge in there."

"Very good! The Drum Bridge."

"I couldn't climb this the last time, Daddy."

"Well, it's been a while. The bridge shrank."

"Ha-ha! Do all bridges in Japan look like this?"

"Only in fancy gardens."

"Do they have bridges like the Golden Gate?"

"They've got longer ones. But ours is the most famous bridge in the world. How about green tea and *manju*?"

"Goody. I love dumplings. There's a gift shop in the teahouse too."

"What a memory!"

"Maybe they have a name tag with my name on it."

"You already have a pretty silver locket I gave you."

"A name tag, Daddy, it's different. You know, a little license plate or bracelet with your name on it. Everybody has one, but there's never anything for Yuriko."

"Trinkets, trinkets all around . . ."

"See, Daddy, nothing with my name on it."

"Look, Sweetheart, a *sumi-e* demonstration's going on."

"What's that?"

"Japanese ink painting."

"He's really good, isn't he?" she said.

"He's a master," Father whispered.

The man looked at the father, then at Yuriko.

"What's your name, young lady?" he asked.

"Yuriko."

"A lovely name, *The Child of the Lily . . .*" The artist quickly drew a lily, and said, "A little present for Yuriko-san."

"Oh, thank you! *Arigato gozaimasu!*"

"He just gave it to me, Daddy! And he painted so fast. He must be very famous."

"Look at you. It's a treasure, and you only wanted a name tag. And I'm very proud of you, Sweetheart, you thanked him in Japanese."

"And this is my name, isn't it?"

"Good memory! It says, 'for Yuriko-san.'"

"I'm going to learn to write it."

"Do you think he gives paintings to everybody?"

"Only to very special persons, I think. I'll have it framed —
for your inspiration. All right, let's get cracking."

"About what?"

"Don't you want to have a look at *the* bridge?"

"Oh, I almost forgot."

But when they got there, a thick fog sat cold and wet on the bridge.

"It's not fair! What good is a famous bridge if you can't see it!"

"Well, maybe it's good you can't see it today."

"Are you being mean, Daddy?"

"Not at all. It makes you use your imagination."

Back home, Yuriko flopped on the couch.

"We already drew the bridge in kindergarten, Daddy. And all the kids are doing the same thing now!"

"So you want an ordinary name, but you want to do something different from everyone else in art. I like the second part a lot."

"Daddy!" Yuriko complained.

"Okay, let's take a cookie break."

"A foggy day in London Town . . ." Yuriko sang. *Tap, tap, tap,* she tapped the beat on her glass. "A foggy day in San Francisco . . ."

"Are you abusing your chopsticks again?"

"Daddy, do you have any cotton?"

"Umm . . . I have an old cushion that's got cotton in it."

"Do you have a big cardboard box?"

"Some in the garage."

"May I borrow your pocketknife?"

"How much of this do you need?"

"Just a little more. This box is perfect."

"I think you'd better let me use that knife. So what's with the chopsticks?"

"Kudo-san said I could play with them."

"All right, tap away . . . start up your recycling station."

On Sunday, Yuriko stayed in her room all morning.

"Are you all right? You're not in bed, are you?" Father asked in the hallway.

"I'm not sick! Don't come in!"

"Just checking . . . I won't snitch your chopsticks."

At lunchtime, Yuriko didn't say anything. Then she returned to her room.

At three o'clock, Father asked through the door, "Do you want your snack?"

"You can come in, Daddy," Yuriko answered.

"What in the . . . Wow!"

"Do you like it?"

"The Golden Gate in the fog! Who would've thought of it! Absolutely wonderful! But wait a second, who's the artist? What name are you going to put on it?"

"I made it. I'm putting my name on it."

"Michelle?"

"No! Yuriko."

"That's my favorite daughter!"

On Monday morning, Father helped Yuriko take her artwork to school.
"How original! It's fabulous, Yuriko!" Ms. Hobbs exclaimed.

As Father left, Yuriko asked, "Daddy, will you take me to Japan someday?"
"Now, that'll be the best trip ever!" Father said.

Some years later, they did go to Japan, and they had the most wonderful time together.